look ○ listen ○

my farm

Rod Campbell

Collins
An Imprint of HarperCollins*Publishers*

"Cock-a-doodle-doo," goes the cockerel.

The hen is pecking in the yard.

The cows are waiting to be milked.

The pigs are having their breakfast.

The sheep are in the field
eating grass.

Sam the farm dog looks after the sheep.

The ducks are paddling on the pond.

The geese honk and hiss when they are cross.

The farm cat looks after her kittens.

The horses are in the stable.

BEAUTY

cockerel
hen
cow
pig
sheep
dog
duck
goose
cat
horse

First published in Great Britain
by Collins Children's Division,
part of HarperCollins Publishers Limited.

3 5 7 9 10 8 6 4 2

The author asserts the moral right to be
identified as the author of the work.
© Rod Campbell 1995

isbn 0 00 100646 0 (book & tape pack)